THE SHADOW THIEVES

A SHORT STORY

ALEXANDRIA BLAELOCK

Also by Alexandria Blaelock

SHORT STORY COLLECTIONS
The Haunting of Hayward Hall
Lovelorn, Lovestruck and Love at First Sight
Common or Garden Variety Heroes
Case Files of the Wilkinson Detective Agency

FICTION
That Love Nonsense

MS BLAELOCK'S BOOKS
Stress Free Dinner Parties
Signature Wardrobe Planning
Holistic Personal Finance
Minimally Viable Housekeeping
Planning a Life Worth Living

A SELECTION OF AVAILABLE SHORT STORIES
Alma's Grace
Balancing the Book
Bygone Boyfriend
Fate in Your Hands
Kiss of Death
Lady of the Looking Glass
Life in the Security Directorate
Love in the Security Directorate
Morning Star, Evening Star, Superstar
Needy Bitch
Payton's Run
Secret Singer
Shining Star
Ship in a Bottle
Simone Says Hands in the Air
The Day the Schedule Broke

THE SHADOW THIEVES

A SHORT STORY

ALEXANDRIA BLAELOCK

BlueMere Books
MELBOURNE, AUSTRALIA

For permission requests, please contact
enquiries@bluemerebooks.com.

Ordering Information:
Discounts are available on quantity purchases. For details, contact orders@bluemerebooks.com.

The Shadow Thieves/Alexandria Blaelock
paperback ISBN: 978-1-925749-78-6
digital ISBN: 978-1-925749-79-3

BlueMere Books
www.bluemerebooks.com

THE SHADOW THIEVES

I t's funny how ordinarily most major events
start when you come down to it.

Like when I first heard about the shadow
thieves, though at the time we didn't know what
they were. Or for that matter, that they existed.

I was working in the Archives.

Now, don't let anyone tell you that Records
Management is an easy job.

It's hard physical labour.

You're always on the go, picking up and
carrying files in a room where they arrive in a
constant barrage.

The sound of their capsules whooshing and
rattling overhead through the pneumatic tubes
and landing with a clatter and burst of air in the
bins is deafening.

Even with the felt lining.

And despite the constant gusts of wind, the
Archive smells stale, because the air is
compressed, not fresh.

And the "fresh" air pumped in from outside
has chemicals added to kill bugs and slow the
paper's rate of decay.

Plus, the lights are kept dim to prevent deterioration of the text.

During your first few weeks in there, you're covered in bruises from head to toe where you keep walking into the racks and bins.

Most new clerks dropped files, and when the papers fell out, they just shoved them back any old how 'cause they couldn't see which sheet went in which file.

Not that you're allowed to read them anyway - they're State Secrets, and the Archivists are kept busy checking and double-checking files as they go out and refiling odd papers correctly.

You should've heard them complain when someone Upstairs didn't write the correct file information on the papers.

You'd think it was a hanging offence.

Then again, in those days, maybe it was.

I'll tell you a secret, different parts of the Archives smell different to other parts, depending on the paper stock and inks they used at the time.

I used to love the smell of the really old vellum section until I found out it's made of treated calf skin.

Made me feel a bit sick, but I suppose they ate the cow, and if it wasn't a book it would have been shoes instead.

I think if I were a cow, I'd rather be a book, gently cared for on a shelf than having people walk all over me.

My very favourites were the files from last century, but old Mr Cox preferred the century before. Reminded him of his youth I expect.

I heard he'd spent almost his entire life in the Archive and it'd made him a bit mad.

That'd be the chemical additives.

Maybe that's why they don't let you spend more than a year or two down there anymore.

Young people today don't know how lucky they are. Though I suppose old Mr Cox would have said the same about me.

In fact, I think the only reason they don't use criminal labour is because of the State Secrets.

Anyway, one of the sections had been damaged by the bombing, and we had to pack up and move all the files so they could make repairs.

Then we'd have to move them back and unpack them, but that's a story for another day.

It was urgent, well more urgent than usual, so we'd been working twelve-hour shifts, from 7 am to 7 pm.

I'd been packing boxes one by one, then carrying them over to the Archivist Department, and stacking them so they could review the files and restore them where necessary.

I was taking my tea break in the morning, though I'm not convinced what I was drinking was actually tea, and I've no idea what the biscuits were made of.

But it was nice to sit and rest, to close my eyes and put my feet up for a moment seeing as no one was looking.

The radio was playing quietly in the background. I'm not sure what caught my attention, but suddenly I was listening carefully to the plummy voice of the newsreader.

"Detectives were called to investigate the suspicious death of a young man in Northbridge last night. The body was discovered in an Ellington Street property around seven-thirty pm. A police spokesman said the exact circumstances of the death were yet to be established, and urged anyone with information to contact their local station."

Now I lived in a boarding house in Ellington Street Northbridge at the time, but with the overtime, I'd been kipping in a nearby air raid shelter because the trams stopped at dusk and I was too tired and scared to walk back in the dark.

When you hear about the war, you don't generally hear much about the day-to-day inconvenience and terrors for those left at home - not really calm but carrying on regardless.

The blackouts and bombing were the perfect conditions for serious crimes like murder, rape, assault and theft to flourish in the darkness.

Not to mention that rationing encouraged fraud, forgery and black-market trading, though you didn't need to worry quite so much about your immediate personal safety when it came to those. Only long-term exposure to whatever the food was cut with.

As if whatever it was extended or substituted with wasn't enough in the first place.

My mother was particularly paranoid about rape, and the consequent potential to be thought no better than "she" ought to be.

She taught me to be afraid too, so when I say I slept in an air raid shelter, I mean dozed a little with one eye open.

Then there was that thing about using public toilets and being kidnapped for the white sex trade. Or picking up something nasty from the toilet seat like happened to so many soldiers abroad.

I guess that's the universal problem all country girls face when they go to work in a Big City like London that's too far away to go home at the end of the day.

Realistically, local thugs were just one more thing on top of the bombing so you never really slept anyway.

In those days, to learn and practice self-defence was only slightly less scandalous than being raped, more's the pity.

I don't know what we were supposed to do when the "bloody Huns" invaded.

Depend on their decency and honour I expect.

Bah!

So after hearing this news report, I decided two things:

1. To sleep in the Archive barracks, and
2. To find some kind of unarmed self-defence class.

But first, I wanted to nip back to my digs to see whether the nameless young man was someone I knew and really hoped was okay.

And that meant asking old Mr Cox for permission, and quite frankly, I found him terrifying.

For one thing he was very old.

His ears were the size of saucers with gobs of hair growing out of them. When he didn't hear you, he'd cup them in one giant paw, demanding "eh?" until you ended up shouting whatever private request you had.

His nicotine stained teeth were long, and straight and seemed to gnash of their own accord. Perhaps to get away from the odour of his breath.

And his watery blue eyes seemed to look around you rather than at you, as if you were some invention of his mad, fevered imagination.

"Mr Cox, sir. I need to get back to my boarding house today, may I leave at the regular time?"

He peered at me for what seemed like a long time, then nodded once in the affirmative.

I bowed slightly back, and scarpered before he could change his mind.

Of course, once I was around the corner out of sight I leaned, shaking, on the wall, breathing as deeply as if I'd run a mile in a minute getting away from the Huns.

I had the idea that he'd been assessing me as I fled, though I couldn't say what for, or what outcome I feared the most. Was death better or worse than rape?

Or was it possible that he saw me for what I was, a naive country girl, and was therefore concerned about my safety?

Or did he think I was young and pretty and have the kind of designs on me my mother worried about?

Urrrgggghhhh!

Shuddering reflexively, I went back to my station.

I worked steadily for another three hours, took a quick lunch break, and worked through until five.

Then, hoping no one would notice, quietly left the office and ran for the tram.

Walking down Ellington Street from the tram stop, you could be forgiven for thinking the War was a nightmare you'd just woken from.

It's funny how I always think of the war in sepia and white, even though I was there and it was as full colour then as the view from my window is now.

Too many old newsreels I expect.

The yellow late Summer sun shone in the bright blue sky as always, and a light, cool breeze blew through the fragrant pink Camellia hedges.

Birds sang high in the treetops, not quite obscuring the sound of children playing in a nearby garden.

It was as bucolic as a suburban street can get.

Well, at least until you turned the dogleg and saw the piles of rubble and bombed out houses.

And smelled the brick dust and bits of rotting bodies that hadn't been found and disposed of.

But we'd been lucky so far, touch wood.

As I walked down the street, nothing much seemed to have changed from when I was last there. It was only a week or so, but aside from murder, a lot can happen in a day.

There wasn't an obvious police presence, though given it was wartime, there wasn't actually much of a local constabulary to be present anyway.

Oddly, I found myself relaxing as I approached the house; a beautiful old Victorian mid-terrace, not too badly damaged by the war.

It mightn't be safe in the literal sense of the word, but it had become my home.

The existence of the other boarders gave me a sense of security, offered a choice of bridge partners and gave me plenty to write home to mother about.

The meals weren't bad either.

Somehow my landlady, Mrs Sumner (widow, as she described herself) managed our ration coupons well enough to stay well stocked with butter, sugar and meat.

Though looking back, I think she must've had "friends" helping her out.

Despite the wartime privations, she remained cheerful, beautiful and vivacious.

A charming host who never seemed to run short of alcohol, lipstick or stockings.

Or body fat.

But when I opened the door, she was uncharacteristically slovenly and all in a dither.

She wasn't wearing lipstick and her hair was escaping the scarf she'd covered it with. She'd missed one of her arms with her apron strap and it dangled loosely from the opposite shoulder.

"Oh, Miss Phillips," she said, "I'm so glad to see you."

"Is everything all right Mrs Sumner?"

"I'm really not sure, we've lost young Mr Chambers."

I felt my heart sink. "Mr Chambers on the third floor?"

"Yes that's right. When he didn't come down to supper last night, I went to fetch him, but he was gone."

"Gone?"

"Yes, gone. And not a mark on him."

"Oh gone. You mean dead." My heart broke a little at the news.

Mrs Sumner frowned, "of course that's what I mean. Did you think he'd done a bunk?"

"I'm so sorry Mrs Sumner. It's just so hard to believe."

And it really was.

He was handsome, funny and lively. I'd never met anyone as alive as Nathan Chambers.

I'd fondly imagined we'd grow close during the war, and marry shortly after.

We'd live long and happy lives, in a lovely rose entwined country cottage with our have bright, beautiful children.

Of all the things I lost during the war, I regret losing him, and that potential life the most.

"Yes, it is," she continued, "I've been struggling with it all day."

"I'm sure it's been difficult for you."

"Yes.

"On top of the shock of finding the body, there was dealing with the Police traipsing muck all over the house and getting in the way.

"I hardly got a wink of sleep all night, and by the time I got to the butcher the queue was around the block and all I could get was something masquerading as mince!"

She made it sound like the tortures of hell, but actually she was very lucky to come away with any meat at all.

I wouldn't have bothered joining a queue that long, I'd have assumed the shop'd be empty by the time I got to the front.

"I'm so sorry, that sounds like an awful day Mrs Sumner."

"Thank you dear, it was.

"But you know what's been bugging me all day? When the Police carried him out, I didn't see his shadow. There was no shadow."

She grabbed my arm and looked up at me, "how could there be no shadow?"

"That's absurd! Of course he had a shadow, it's just that with all the confusion, you didn't see it."

"That's what I thought at first too. But they walked behind the hall lamp! They walked right between it and the wall, and the shadow stretcher was empty! I don't understand how there could be no shadow."

She sighed and rubbed her eyes as I, doubting her sanity, tried to think of something reassuring to say.

"Look, you've had a bit of a shock, and it's been a long and difficult day for you. Let me make you a nice hot cup of tea."

She put her hands in the small of her back, and grunting, stretched before twisting out her shoulders. I'm sure I heard her bones crack.

"Thank you Miss Phillips, but I still have a lot to get done.

"Aside from making supper, the Police say I can pack Mr Chamber's belongings and send them back to his relatives, though Lord knows where the money's coming from for that."

I was a little bit in shock myself, but this seemed like the perfect opportunity to poke about in his things, and maybe save something for myself, so I said, "I'll do the packing for you if you like Mrs Sumner."

She patted my arm, "you're a good girl Miss Phillips," and disappeared through the door to the back stairs.

Which I took to be her grateful assent.

In retrospect, regardless of the circumstances, I'm a little surprised she allowed a single woman to enter a single man's room, let alone touch his things. But she did.

I suppose she was preoccupied with losing his ration card and income, so her primary concern was to have the room cleared and ready to let as quickly as possible.

But you know what? During Wartime, you see and smell much worse things than a man's empty underpants.

His room was next to mine, and like mine, was smallish, sparse, neat and clean. The nearby bombing had shaken some plaster from the ceiling, but the wallpaper held the walls together just fine.

The room smelled so strongly of Old Spice that it was almost as if he'd just left and would be back any moment.

I closed my eyes and swallowed the sob that was threatening to stick in my throat.

Of course there were people who just couldn't deal with the daily tragedies of wartime, but I wasn't one of them. Though that evening was the closest I ever came to not getting on with it.

Young people make fun of us and our stiff upper lips, but really, all you could do was stiffen your lips to stop the snivelling coming out.

If one of us started blubbering it set everyone else off, and given we all had it tough, it just didn't do to let others down with your lack of self-control.

So, I pressed my lips together, took his small canvas suitcase down from the top of the wardrobe, and laid it gently on the single bed.

What with rationing and all, it took next to no time to take his folded clothes from the dresser and pack them in the case.

A chipped saucer on top of the dresser held his watch, cuff links and some shirt studs.

The Art Deco Styled watch was as beautiful as it was unusual.

The rectangular face was branded LeCoultre, and its gleaming gold and pristine glass suggested it was new. The back signed "Cased and Timed in the USA."

I held it in my hands, marvelling at its perfection. I wondered how seemingly dirt-poor Nathan Chambers came to have a brand-new American luxury watch in his London digs.

And then I remembered the watch I'd seen him wearing was round, steel and completely undistinguished.

The kind of workhorse watch that was common among the men of my acquaintance.

And I wondered where it was.

I'm sorry to say I thought about keeping the watch, but I just couldn't do it.

It seemed the kind of thing I'd never be able to adequately provenance. People would always wonder how someone like me came by an expensive watch like that no matter what story I came up with.

I put it with the other jewellery and toiletries in his wash bag, and packed that in his case, along with one small tear I couldn't hold back when I saw he was only half way through a Dennis Wheatley novel and would never learn the ending.

The book seemed a much better souvenir, so I "accidentally" dropped it behind the headboard to keep for later.

I still have it now.

After the funeral, I visited his grave and told him how it ended. Just in case he wondered.

Once I'd finished with the case, I took it downstairs to the kitchen.

The kitchen was a mess, the breakfast dishes hadn't been done, and it looked like the fire in the stove had gone out.

Mrs Sumner was sitting at the kitchen table next to her shopping, which was still in its string carry bag, resting in a pool of meat blood that had soaked through the paper.

A fly buzzed as it tried to escape through the lightwell.

She was cradling her face in her hands. It was almost as if she'd fallen and couldn't get up.

"Are you all right Mrs Sumner?"

She jumped, "Oh, Miss Phillips, are you done already?"

She really didn't look well, so I asked again, "are you all right?"

"I'm sorry Miss Phillips, I guess I'm just a bit shaken."

We weren't close, but I risked resting my hand on her shoulder in a show of sympathy.

"I mean you get used to seeing bodies on the street, but to find one in your own home, and not a mark on him."

It seemed to me that she must be in shock, so I stoked the fire in the stove (thankfully not fully out) and put the kettle on.

I wanted to get back and rescue the book, but I really didn't think I should leave her as she was just then.

Unlikely that anyone else would be in his room anyway.

While I waited for the kettle to boil, I ran some cold water in the sink, whisked it up with the soap cage, and stacked the breakfast dishes in there.

Once the kettle boiled, I filled up the tea pot and poured the rest into sink.

I set a pink rose decorated cup on a matching saucer in front of her, but she just looked at it.

I'd heard slapping people was the thing to do, but I had the idea if I did that, she'd fall off her chair.

And maybe hurt herself.

And I'd probably be looking for new lodgings.

With seven other residents due home shortly, I was torn between getting supper on the go and getting back to Mr Chamber's room to rescue the book.

And then I had a brain wave.

"Drink this Mrs Sumner, I'll go and strip the bed for you. And when I get back, I'll give you a hand with the supper."

"You're a good girl Miss Phillips."

I felt selfish and guilty for a very short moment, but I pushed the steaming cup closer and nipped back upstairs.

The odd thing was though, that while I was folding the blankets, I noticed a scorch mark, partially concealed by the large purple and blue floral print of the wallpaper.

I thought maybe the lamp had blown and the socket caught fire, but the mark was about waist height, as tall as the dresser.

And nowhere near the socket.

I supposed it was possible for the wires inside the wall to catch fire, but I imagined it more likely the house would burn down than that the wall would scorch.

And I supposed that it might have been there all along, but it seemed fresh in comparison to the faded wallpaper.

It bothered me.

But I wasn't sure who I knew who might know something about it.

Except maybe old Mr Cox, but that was mainly because he was a man.

And having lived his life in the Archive, probably knew stuff.

I was still worried about Mrs Sumner (and my supper), so I quickly threw the book on my bed and hurried downstairs with an armload of sheets to be washed.

She hadn't moved.

Not even to take a sip of tea.

I wanted to ask her if she'd seen the scorch mark, but I had the sense that it was a step too far right now and she'd fall off the edge if I mentioned it.

So I let her sit, staring into space, and bustled about the kitchen making supper - cottage pie.

Because I knew how to make it, it's relatively quick, and makes delicious leftovers.

Which was lucky because it looked like a lot of mince, even for ten people.

I mean nine.

She paid me no mind while I prepped the veg, but the smell of the meat frying started to bring her round, and by the time the pie was ready to go in the oven, she was more or less back to normal.

Or the Mrs Sumner I was used to anyway.

"Oh Miss Phillips, you really are a gem."

"Thank you Mrs Sumner, can I make you another cup of tea?"

"Thank you, but no. You've been busy, and it's time I pulled myself together. You sit and I'll make you one."

She busied herself emptying the pot, and setting aside the leaves to dry out and reuse.

Then made a fresh pot with new, unused leaves.

Not even mixing it with the old.

I felt guilty again, because everything I'd done had been about me, and I hadn't thought about her at all.

But it seemed she appreciated the small few things I'd done since I got home, and the tea was delicious.

It had been such a long since I'd had real tea, and I wasn't going to complain if she wanted to waste it on me.

She'd started to look more like the woman I knew, so perhaps it was more about what she needed right then.

We sat for a while in comfortable silence appreciating "proper" tea.

"Did you know Mr Chambers well?" she asked.

I'm ashamed to say I blushed, "Not very."

"You would have liked to?"

"Yes," blushing even more.

"Do you know what he did for work?"

"No."

"I heard he was in the Secret Service?"

"Secret Service? Goodness! Keep Mum!" I was momentarily stunned.

"Though, how did you find that out?"

Mrs Sumner smiled and tapped the side of her nose.

I wasn't sure if she meant he'd told her or someone else had.

Though probably not him. If he really was a spy, he'd have wanted to keep that secret.

The sun went behind a cloud, and the room dimmed.

"Mrs Sumner, do you think his job could've had anything to do with his death?"

She gasped, "goodness! I hadn't thought of that."

As if looking for a distraction she refilled our cups, frowning. "I guess if you want to delay an investigation, the best way would be to kill the investigator. And these days, no one would be the wiser."

"But how much time could that get you? They'd have to find someone new and bring them up to speed. A week? Two maybe?"

"If you were prepared, a week'd probably be enough to wrap things up and get out."

"I guess a week doesn't give the Bureau much time to catch up with and arrest someone who's determined to get away. Especially if they don't have an available investigator."

"Assuming they know he's dead."

"Wouldn't the police let them know?"

"If Mr Chambers was an undercover spy, how would the police even know? It might be days before his supervisor tries to get in touch."

"Mrs Sumner, did you or the police notice the scorch mark on the wall?"

"Scorch mark? What scorch mark?"

That was a no then.

I took her back up to the room and pointed it out.

"That's odd, I haven't seen that before," she said, crouching and scrubbing at the wall with her index finger.

Which was clean when she looked at it.

"It looks to me, a little like the kind of mark you get when you hold a candle a little too close to the wall."

"I think you're right," she said, "though I haven't given him any candles. Did you see anything in his things that might have made this mark?"

"No. Unless maybe you count shoe polish. Why anyone would go to so much trouble to apply shoe polish to a wall is beyond me."

"Indeed. It's odd all right."

We sat side by side on the bed, looking at the wall.

"Mrs Sumner, I heard on the radio his body was found at seven-thirty pm. Did you see him come home?"

"No. He got back about six, and called out to let me know he'd arrived."

"Was he alone?"

Mrs Sumner frowned for a moment, "He didn't say anything about anyone with him, and I didn't hear anything to suggest he had someone with him. He's always followed the rules before, so I've no reason to suspect him of anything."

"So he arrived home alone, and an hour or so later, he was dead."

We looked at each other.

"Did he say or do anything to suggest he felt unwell?" I asked.

She looked up at the ceiling, trying to remember. "He might have stumbled on the stairs, but I don't really know."

"So something happened to him before he got home, and he died later. Or something happened in this room and he died at the time."

Mrs Sumner nodded once, "makes sense."

"But there was no sign of injury or any kind of attack on his body, and that suggests whatever it was that happened, happened here.

"Very close to his time of death."

She shuddered, "do you think it has something to do with the scorch mark?"

"It seems likely, but I have no idea what could have made that mark."

"I think you're on to something. Some kind of hot thing that took his shadow."

"Like Nana stealing Peter Pan's shadow?"

She laughed, "I think the dog just shut the window and cut it off."

"Oh!

"Did you notice whether the window was open when you came looking for Mr Chambers?"

She frowned again, and then slapped the bed, "it was half open when I first came to find him, but it was closed when I brought the Police back!"

"Are you sure it was closed, and that they didn't close it?"

"Yes. Detective Whatchamacallit asked me about the window."

"And did you come into the room when you found Mr Chambers, or did you just call from the doorway?"

"First, I knocked and called out, then I opened the door and called again. When I still didn't get an answer, I came in.

"He looked peacefully asleep, and I'd half a mind to leave him sleeping, but I didn't want him to miss his meal, so I gave him a little shake.

"He didn't move or acknowledge me, so I checked his pulse."

"And you didn't see anyone, or anything unusual?"

"Not at all."

"Could someone have hidden in the corner or behind the door?"

Mrs Sumner shuddered, "that's a gruesome thought. I didn't turn the light on, just used the light from the hall, so I suppose it's possible someone was hiding in the shadows."

"And that was about seven-thirty, so what happened next?"

"Well. I closed the door as I left the room. I was thinking there was no need for the other residents to see that, then I telephoned the Police. They said they'd send someone around immediately, and they arrived a little after eight."

"And you didn't hear anything to suggest any kind of activity in the room?"

"Not a peep. Mind you, this is the third floor and you don't hear much when you're in the basement do you?"

"I suppose not," I said. "So he and the wall were fine when he came home. But an hour and a half later, the window's open, he's dead, and there's a mark on the wall.

"When the police arrive half an hour after that, the window's closed."

Mrs Sumner looked at her watch, "goodness, look at the time. I'd best get back downstairs and finish the supper before everyone gets home."

I followed her down the stairs, "something else that's odd, there was an expensive American watch on the dresser, but I didn't see any sign of his other watch - the one he wore all the time."

She stopped so abruptly and I almost walked into her, "I only ever saw him with one ordinary watch. Did you put the new one in his case?"

"Yes."

"Then let's get Supper done and take a look at it."

I admit I was impatient. I wanted supper to be over so I could get back to the mystery of what happened to Nathan.

Mrs Sumner, on the other hand, seemed reluctant to let anyone leave the dining room, and was uncharacteristically generous with the wine.

I suppose she was worried in case someone else went to their room and came out dead.

Especially if that someone was her.

Mind you, the talk of the table was about the mysterious death, so I did encourage the conversation to linger on what people had seen and heard.

And I realised, that living in a boarding house was not as much of a guarantee of safety as I had first thought, because:

a) There is something(s) out there that can scale three stories up the front of your house and climb inside your bedroom without being seen, and

b) Despite the creaking wooden floors, threadbare rugs on the floor dampen more noise than you'd expect, and

c) People are not as nosey as I'd imagined, even for wartime.

It sent a chill down my spine.

The only thing I could do was to find and eliminate the somethings, and I had no idea how to do that.

I was also thinking I ought to have closed my bedroom window, and wondering whether I'd be able to sleep without what passes for fresh air in London leaking through an open window.

But eventually, one by one, the lodgers retired to their rooms, and not even the offer of a drink of port was enough to entice them to the lounge for a game of cards.

Perhaps they were unsettled by the death too, and maybe they thought they were safer alone, in their rooms.

Mrs Sumner sat deflated, at the head of the table, so left her there and started clearing it.

I felt quite sorry for her, so I decided to just leave the watch and my Miss Marple investigation where it was.

After all, I was a farm girl, and I didn't know anything about anything.

Realistically there was nothing I could do about Nathan's death or fantastical creatures that scale buildings.

But she roused herself, and started collecting dishes together at her end of the table.

For a moment, I felt a flare of hope, but wilfully quenched it.

Sleeping dogs and all that.

After dropping the dishes back in the kitchen, I bade Mrs Sumner goodnight.

She opened her mouth and raised her hand, but let it drop and wished me a goodnight in return.

The first thing I did when I got back to my room, was firmly close the window before drawing the blackout curtains.

I put the lamp on, and turned to walk back to the door to switch the room light off.

As I turned, I looked at the door.

Trying to decide whether to leave it open. Though I'm not entirely sure whether I thought that would be for an easy get away, or that one of the lodgers might hear a kerfuffle and investigate.

And none of the doors had locks on them anyway.

But despite all our time together, I didn't know any of them besides Nathan very well.

And after the conversation at dinner, I didn't think I could rely on any of them to venture out of their rooms to render assistance.

More likely they'd all hide under their beds trembling.

Assuming they didn't take advantage of the situation to push their own interests.

Mr Morris upstairs, in particular, always made me feel uncomfortable.

Even more than old Mr Cox at the Archive.

Anyway, whatever it was that killed Nathan was slightly less frightening than the lodgers.

It had left his body without a mark, looking for all the world as if he'd died peacefully in his sleep. Not fighting desperately for his life.

In the end, I closed the door, before flipping off the light switch

I changed into my night clothes, and hung my day clothes in the wardrobe.

The day had been physically and emotionally exhausting. I was tired, and perhaps a little overwrought.

On my own, in the "safety" of my room, I sat on my bed facing the wall I shared with Nathan and let the tears come.

I cried and I cried and I cried.

But quietly, because I didn't want anyone to know or investigate.

The increasingly intense aroma of Old Spice I took to be my memories intensifying as I dwelled on them.

I was startled to hear a throat clearing behind me. Especially as I'd made a special effort to secure the window closed.

I leapt off the bed and spun towards the window at the speed of light.

To face a plumpish middle-aged toff in a dinner suit, leaning on a gold topped black walking stick, wearing his top hat at a jaunty angle.

I rubbed my eyes, but he was still there.

So, I pinched myself, and had a sore arm to prove that I was quite awake.

He tapped his stick on the floor a couple of times, "if you've quite finished," he said with an American accent.

I don't mind telling you my heart about stopped of its own accord, this "man" was obviously what killed Nathan.

"I left my wrist watch here last night. I picked up this monstrosity by accident," he waved his arm, "but it really doesn't go with my outfit. I don't suppose you've seen it at all have you?"

"You killed Nathan!"

"Oh, is that what his name was?"

How could he be so casual about killing him?

Not that I knew who his people were, but what I'd seen back home was that rich people like him had no regard for anyone other than more rich people like him.

Assuming they had any regard for anyone at all.

We just existed to farm their fields, cook their food and keep their houses tidy. The less noticeable the better.

Even then I knew it wasn't sensible to bait him, but I was really quite angry.

"You killed someone and you don't know anything about him?"

"Be sensible girl, I'm not going to kill someone I know, am I?"

I started taking a backwards step towards the door, hoping it wouldn't look as though I was trying to escape, "but why?"

"To be honest, I didn't mean to kill him," he said, and disappeared.

His voice continued behind me.

Between me and the door.

"But he'd been asking too many questions, and he just wouldn't let go.

"In the end, he just left me no choice."

I started turning to face him, "so he was a spy then."

He laughed, and reached out to catch me, "my dear girl, you have no idea."

I unwittingly looked into his eyes, and at that point, lost control of my body. I was trying with every inch of my fibre to pull away, but my body wouldn't obey my commands.

I couldn't even look away from him.

He laughed, "you're a feisty one, aren't you? I'm going to enjoy this." He bent his head to kiss me, and I was squirming and wriggling on the inside, desperate to get away but powerless to move.

And there we were, for all intents and purposes, locked in a passionate embrace.

Which made it a bad time for Mrs Sumner to open the door on us, saying "Miss Phillips, I wanted to apologise..."

And then, "good Lord," when she realised what she was looking at.

Which made it a very good time, because she distracted him, and I was able to twist free.

He pointed a finger at her, and a jet of blue fire shot from the tip cutting across her arm at the wrist.

She yelped in pain as her arm fell to her side, and something came loose and fell to the floor.

She clutched her elbow, "my arm!"

It was enough to neutralise her for a moment, so he turned his attention back to me.

But I was watching his body, not his eyes, so when I saw him raise his arm towards me, I knew I didn't have much time.

Gambling he knew nothing about our football, I threw myself at his feet in a low and dirty tackle which overbalanced him.

Blue fire arced overhead as he fell backwards.

Copying my football hero, I rolled myself on my back and flipped up and across his body, hoping to weight him down.

But I was just a slip of a girl in those days, one that rarely got enough to eat, and I was no match for him.

I couldn't stop him getting up, but I kept a firm grip on his firing arm as he struggled to throw me off.

Mrs Sumner seemed to get over the shock of whatever he'd done to her, and grabbed at his other side, bringing him down to the ground again.

Grunting with effort, he struggled frantically to get his arm free, but only succeeded in shooting random bolts of light around the room.

Mrs Sumner stayed low, and well out of its way.

Small or not, I'd grown up on a farm, and I was more or less used to manhandling pigs, cows or sheep into line.

Holding his arm, and leveraging my toes against the floor, I pushed it back in a way I hoped would break it.

He screeched, and while I'm not sure whether I broke it or not, he fell still.

Mrs Sumner and I lay still for a moment, trying to get our breath back while holding the motionless body down.

Then we looked at each other and silently agreed we could risk letting go to take a look.

Aside from a scorch mark across his face, he looked peaceful.

I gave the scorch a hard poke, but there was no response.

Mrs Sumner took his pulse and shook her head.

"How's your arm?" I asked.

She rubbed her arm, "arms's fine. but I've no feeling in my hand."

I nodded once, then staggered over to the door, and flipped the light switch.

We both gasped.

The ceiling, walls and floor were striped with scorch marks.

I shut the door.

In the event that another lodger came to see what was going on, I didn't want them seeing the body or the scorch marks.

Something dark and light, like a shadow, fluttered across the floor in the gust of air created when the door closed.

Mrs Sumner made a grab for it, and it seemed she caught it, but it sort of evaporated and slipped through her fingers.

"Well," she said, "I expect we know what made the scorch marks then."

We both giggled a little hysterically.

"Should we call the police?" I asked.

She thought for a moment. "I really don't want to deal with that lot again today. Do you think we could get him back out the window and call them in the morning?"

"Are you sure you're up to it?"

"I'll manage."

Whatever else the American had done; without her hand she couldn't use her arm for much more than balancing the body.

Which was very heavy.

But somehow, we managed to get it over to the window.

I turned the lamp off and opened the blackout curtains a crack. Dusk seeped in the gap. I didn't need to say it, but I did, "we'll have to wait until it's darker."

Mrs Sumner sighed, "I think I need a brandy in the meantime. Would you care to join me Miss Phillips?"

"I think that's an excellent idea."

We trudged back down to the kitchen, where Mrs Sumner fetched a couple of glasses and poured a generous slosh into each.

After finished coughing out my first sip, I said, "Mrs Sumner, I think after all this, you might start calling me Sadie."

"And you may call me Agnes."

We smiled at each other.

"I don't suppose we need to look at the watch now do we?"

I shook my head slowly. "So, what do we do with it all now?"

"I s'pose we just send it back to his family and let them worry about it."

We sat quietly together, each in our own thoughts, so we were both startled by the front door bell ringing, followed by urgent heavy knocking on the door.

"Do you think someone knows what we did?" I asked.

"I doubt it," as the knock came again. "I suppose I should go answer that."

I picked up a heavy pan and followed her up the stairs, hiding just around the corner as she approached the door calling "who is it?"

The muffled answer seemed sufficient as she opened the door to reveal a middle-aged man in a beige trench coat, brown utility suit and bowler hat.

Ridiculously, his obvious Englishness made us feel we could trust him.

I came out from the stairs, holding the pan behind my back as he introduced himself as Mr Sutcliffe, claiming to be Nathan's boss and asking politely if he could see him.

Mrs Sumner and I looked at each other, and she explained he'd died and been taken away by the police.

"I see," said Mr Sutcliffe, "he was working on a project, and I wonder if I might see his room for a moment.

We looked at each other again, and she said, "follow me."

I fell in behind as they climbed the stairs.

She opened Nathan's door and turned the light on for him.

He looked around the room, and immediately walked across the room to the scorch mark. Mrs Sumner nudged me, but I shook my head and mouthed "not yet."

"Any idea what made the mark?" he asked.

"Yes," said Mrs Sumner, I glared at her but she ignored me "come next door and I'll show you."

She threw open my door and turned the light on.

The American was where we'd left him, and Mr Sutcliffe sucked in his breath as he saw the damage.

"And, er, how did you, er, disarm the, er creature?"

Mrs Sumner, throwing caution to the wind, pointed at me, "she threw its arm back and it… And it scorched its own face, and its light went out. It was kind of like it had cut its own head off."

"Interesting," said Mr Sutcliffe, "we've been trying to work out how to kill them."

"Now listen here young man," Mrs Sumner said, "I think you'd better tell me what's going on right now."

"Just one moment."

He ducked back into Nathan's room, and we heard him pulling drawers out of the dresser. We got back just in time to see him pull a file from the floor under the bottom of the chest. He folded it in half and shoved it inside the pocket of his coat.

"Did either of you get caught by the fire?"

"It caught Mrs Sumner across the wrist."

"I'll need to use your telephone," he said heading for the stairs.

"What's going on?" Mrs Sumner asked his disappearing back.

She took a step after him, and somehow tripped on the edge of the rug and fell. I picked her up, and pulled her behind me as I chased Mr Sutcliffe down the stairs.

We missed the conversation, but when he saw me half carrying Mrs Sumner, he dropped the handset back in the cradle and took a step forward to help, picking her up and carrying her into the lounge.

"Do you have any brandy?" he asked.

"I'll get some," I replied and rushed down the stairs to grab the bottle and glasses before running back up again, almost tripping on the last step.

It sure had been a long day.

When I arrived in the room, he was pushing a pin into her arm.

"No," she said.

I was about to protest, but he held his hand up, and moved the pin a little higher up her arm, "no," she said again. A little higher and she squealed.

"Right, the brandy please."

I poured us each a glass, and he told Mrs Sumner to drink it down quickly. She did so, and gestured at me to refill it.

"We call them the Shadow Thieves," he said, because they leave clean bodies without shadows. We think they live off the energy in them, but we don't know how it works."

We nodded.

"We do know they cut the shadows off with the blue fire they shoot from their hands. It's as if it opens a wound and your life leaks out of.

"We've found we can stop the leak if we excise the affected limb before the numbness spreads."

Mrs Sumner clutched at her elbow, a little higher than where the feeling ended.

"I've called for backup, and going by the rate of spread, we should be able to remove your arm, cauterise the wound and save your life.

She gulped.

When the doorbell rang again, he leaped to his feet and opened the door to what looked like an ambulance crew.

Quickly and quietly, they were in the lounge, injecting Mrs Sumner with something and helping her onto a stretcher. She was in the ambulance and they were on their way just a few minutes later.

"And how are you getting on, Mr Sutcliffe asked me.

It had been quite a day, and the brandy was kicking in, so I just shrugged.

"What are you going to do about the American?"

"Was it American?"

I nodded.

"That's interesting given the Americans are more or less encouraging us to come to terms with Hitler.

"I wonder if it was working for the Nazis or just for itself."

I shrugged again, "it didn't do much more than complain it had lost its wrist watch."

Mr Sutcliffe unsuccessfully attempted to smother a laugh.

It made me start laughing, and soon I was laughing as hard as I'd been crying before, and he was patting my back and trying to calm me down.

But eventually the humour died, and Mr Sutcliffe cleared his throat.

"There's another team on the way to collect the body and take it to out lab."

"And what happens then?"

"Then your life goes back to normal."

"Is there such a thing as normal after being attacked by a petulant Shadow Thief?" I wondered out loud.

"As normal as possible anyway."

"I'm not sure I can do normal anymore."

"Well you're the only person we know of who's brought down a Shadow Thief, if you're not looking for normal, I'm sure we could find a place for you at the Bureau."

I wasn't exactly sure how I felt about his offer, but I was even less sure how I felt about facing old Mr Cox again.

"Take some time to think about it," he said as there was another knock on the door.

I stayed in my lounge chair and left him to open the door and take care of the body.

Closing my eyes, thinking about the day, and what might be next.

Waking with a start when Mr Sutcliffe shook my shoulder.

I was suddenly aware I was lying in an undignified sprawl in my nightgown, with nothing to protect my modesty.

"We're done here," he said. "I'll let you get some rest."

I clutched my nightgown around me, "I'm not sure that's possible right now. Even though you've taken that creature out of my room."

"Nothing can harm you now," he said, "and I think you'll find that once you put your head down, you'll get back to sleep in no time at all."

As it turned out he was right, though I got fully dressed before lying on the bed and pulling the blankets over me.

Mrs Sumner was confined to hospital for a month, and despite the pain was generally in good spirits.

A constant stream of visitors left flowers, chocolates and fruit, some of which she shared with me.

I stayed on with her when I changed jobs and started working at the Bureau, and when she died, she left me this house.

So, I opened it up for new recruits like you to stay in, and here you are being so kind to sit and listen to an old lady's stories.

Yes, my dear, I'd love another cup of tea, and perhaps another biscuit

Oh no dear, I think it's too late for another story, you've got to get up early in the morning and go save the City.

I'll rest well knowing you're out there taking of things.

THE END

ABOUT THE AUTHOR

Alexandria Blaelock writes stories, some of them for *Ellery Queen's Mystery Magazine* and *Pulphouse Fiction Magazine*. She's also written five self-help books applying business techniques to personal matters like getting dressed, cleaning house, and feeding your friends.

She lives in a forest because she enjoys birdsong, the scent of gum leaves and the sun on her face. When not telecommuting to parallel universes from her Melbourne based imagination, she watches K-dramas, talks to animals, and drinks Campari. At the same time.

Discover more at www.alexandriablaelock.com.